To Bossy and Daisy —D. L.

For my brother, Dave —M. W.

With special thanks to
Mary Kate Castellani, for her
udder enthusiasm for this book
from day one

Text copyright © 2013 by David LaRochelle
Illustrations copyright © 2013 by Mike Wohnoutka
All rights reserved. No part of this book may be reproduced or transmitted in any form or by any means,
electronic or mechanical, including photocopying, recording, or by any information storage and retrieval system,
without permission in writing from the publisher.

First published in the United States of America in October 2013
by Walker Books for Young Readers, an imprint of Bloomsbury Publishing, Inc.
www.bloomsbury.com

For information about permission to reproduce selections from this book, write to
Permissions, Walker BFYR, 1385 Broadway, New York, New York 10018
Bloomsbury books may be purchased for business or promotional use. For information on bulk purchases please contact
Macmillan Corporate and Premium Sales Department at specialmarkets@macmillan.com

Library of Congress Cataloging-in-Publication Data
LaRochelle, David.
Moo! / by David LaRochelle ; illustrated by Mike Wohnoutka.
pages   cm
Summary: When Cow gets her hooves on the farmer's car, she takes it for a wild ride through the country.
ISBN 978-0-8027-3409-9 (hardcover) • ISBN 978-0-8027-3410-5 (reinforced)
[1. Cows—Fiction. 2. Automobile driving—Fiction. 3. Behavior—Fiction. 4. Humorous stories.]
I. Wohnoutka, Mike, illustrator. II. Title.
PZ7.L3234Mo 2013   [E]—dc23   2013007463

Art created with gouache paint
Typeset in Century Gothic
Book design by Regina Flath

Printed in China by C&C Offset Printing Co., Ltd., Shenzhen, Guangdong
2 4 6 8 10 9 7 5 3 1 (hardcover)
2 4 6 8 10 9 7 5 3 1 (reinforced)

All papers used by Bloomsbury Publishing, Inc., are natural, recyclable products
made from wood grown in well-managed forests. The manufacturing processes
conform to the environmental regulations of the country of origin.

Moo!

David LaRochelle

illustrated by

Mike Wohnoutka

WALKER BOOKS FOR YOUNG READERS
AN IMPRINT OF BLOOMSBURY
NEW YORK   LONDON   NEW DELHI   SYDNEY

Moo.

Moo!

MOO-moo . . .

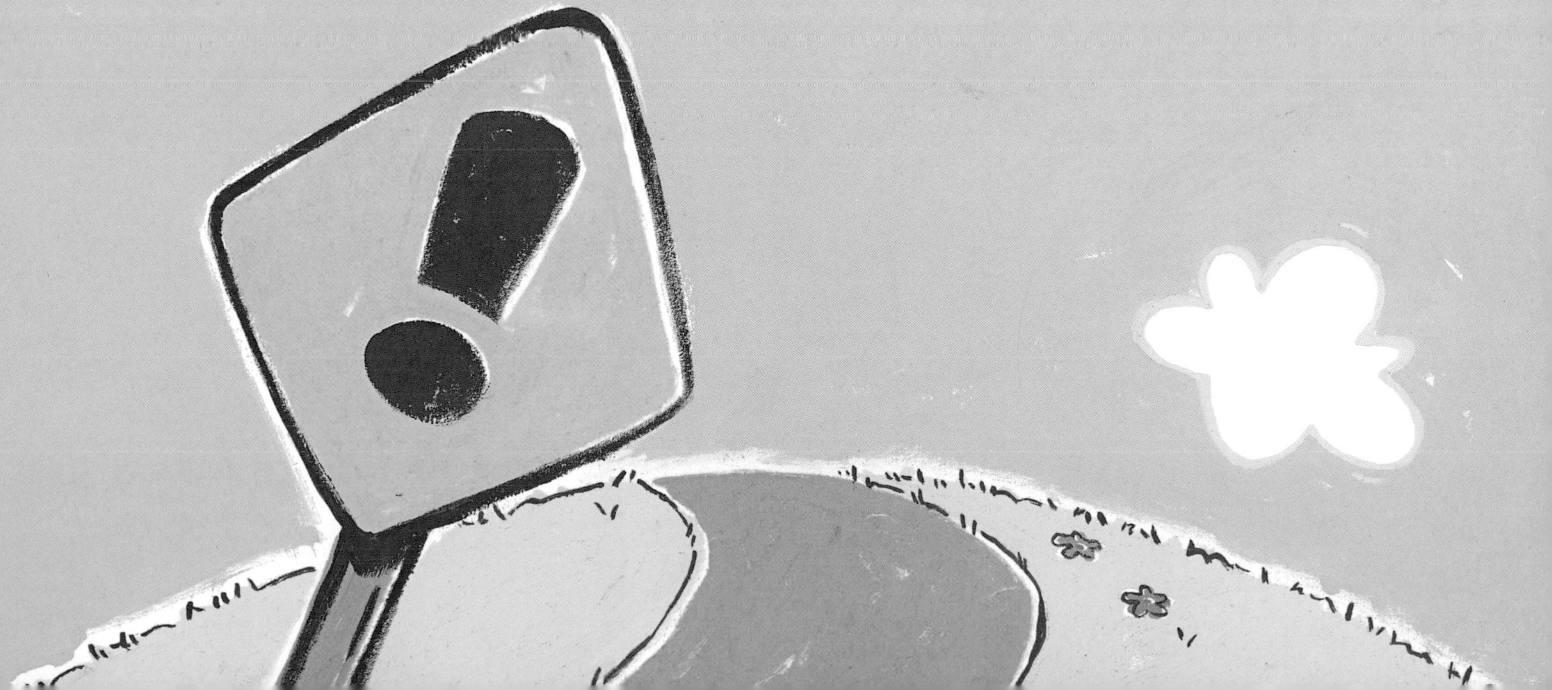

Moo moo!
Moo moo-moo moo!
Moo **moo, moo, moooooo!**
Moooooooooooooo moo.
Moo moo? Moo.
Moo-moo-moo-moo-moo!
Moo moo,
moo moo.
Moo, moo, moo,
MOOO!

Moo.